Aladdin

Miles Kelly

Once upon a time,
a boy called
Aladdin lived
with his mother in
a land called China.

One day a strange
man arrived at
Aladdin's house.
"I am your long-
lost uncle," he said.

He asked Aladdin to help him
find some treasure.

However, the man was really an evil wizard.

He took Aladdin to a dark cave and told him to find a gold lamp that lay inside.

The wizard could only have the lamp if someone else gave it to him.

He took a ring
off his finger
and gave it
to Aladdin.

"This magic
ring will help
you find the lamp,"
he told him.

So Aladdin bravely went into the cave and found the gold lamp.

But, afraid of being trapped inside, he refused to give it to the wizard until he was out of the cave.

"You foolish boy!" shouted the wizard in a rage.

He muttered some magic words and at once a big rock slid across the cave entrance.

Aladdin was trapped!

For two days, Aladdin
was stuck in the dark cave,
very scared. He wondered why
the lamp was so special, and
at last rubbed off some dirt
to get a better look at it.

In a cloud
of smoke
a genie burst from
the lamp!

"Get me out of this cave please," cried Aladdin.

"I am the
genie of
the lamp.
What is it that you wish for?" he boomed.

In a flash, Aladdin was home.

He told his mother all about the wizard and the lamp. After that, they asked the genie for a great many things.

They never wanted for anything.

Some years later, Aladdin saw a princess travelling through the town with her family.

She was charming
and beautiful.
Aladdin
fell in love
with her
at once.

He said to the genie, "Please build me a palace of the finest stone to impress the princess. I wish to marry her."

The genie built Aladdin a dazzling palace. When the princess was asked to visit, she was amazed.

Aladdin and the
princess were
married, watched
by all their friends
and family.

When the wizard heard about the wedding, he realized that Aladdin had escaped from the cave.

He decided to steal the lamp for himself.

Disguised as a
pedlar, he went
to the palace when
Aladdin was away.

He met with the princess. "I'll give you this new lamp for your old lamp," he offered.

The princess didn't know that the old lamp was magic, so she happily handed it to the wizard.

The wizard quickly rubbed the lamp, and then told the genie to move the palace to Africa!

With a sudden flash, the princess, the wizard and the palace vanished.

When Aladdin tried to return home, he was shocked to find the palace had gone.

But he remembered that he still had the wizard's

magic ring.

"Take me to the princess!" he told it. And he was!

Together they made a potion,
which the princess gave to
the wizard.

The potion
made him
fall into a
deep sleep.

Aladdin rushed to take the magic lamp from the wizard. He rubbed it and the genie appeared once more.

"Take me, the princess and the palace back to China!" Aladdin cried.
And they were!

Aladdin and the princess lived **happily** ever after.

And the genie made sure the wizard could never find them again!

He's probably still wandering around the desert!